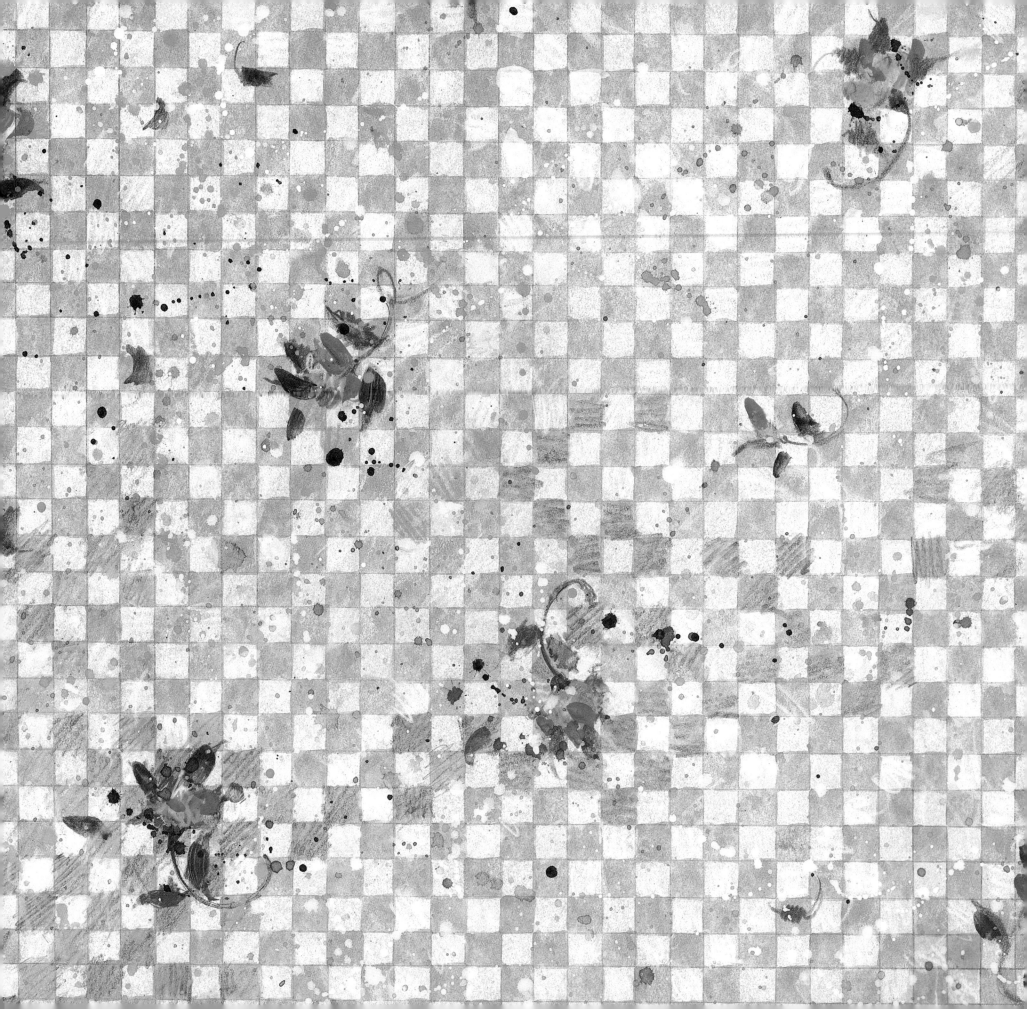

Everyday Angels

Written by
Mark Kimball Moulton

illustrated by
Susan Winget

Lang Books
A Lang Company

Text by Mark kimball Moulton
Illustrations by Susan Winget
©Copyright 2000
All Rights Reserved

Published by Lang Books
A Division of R.A. Lang Card Company, Ltd.
514 Wells St.
Delafield, WI. 53018
800-967-3399
ISBN: 0-7412-0737-0

10 9 8 7 6 5 4 3 2
third Edition

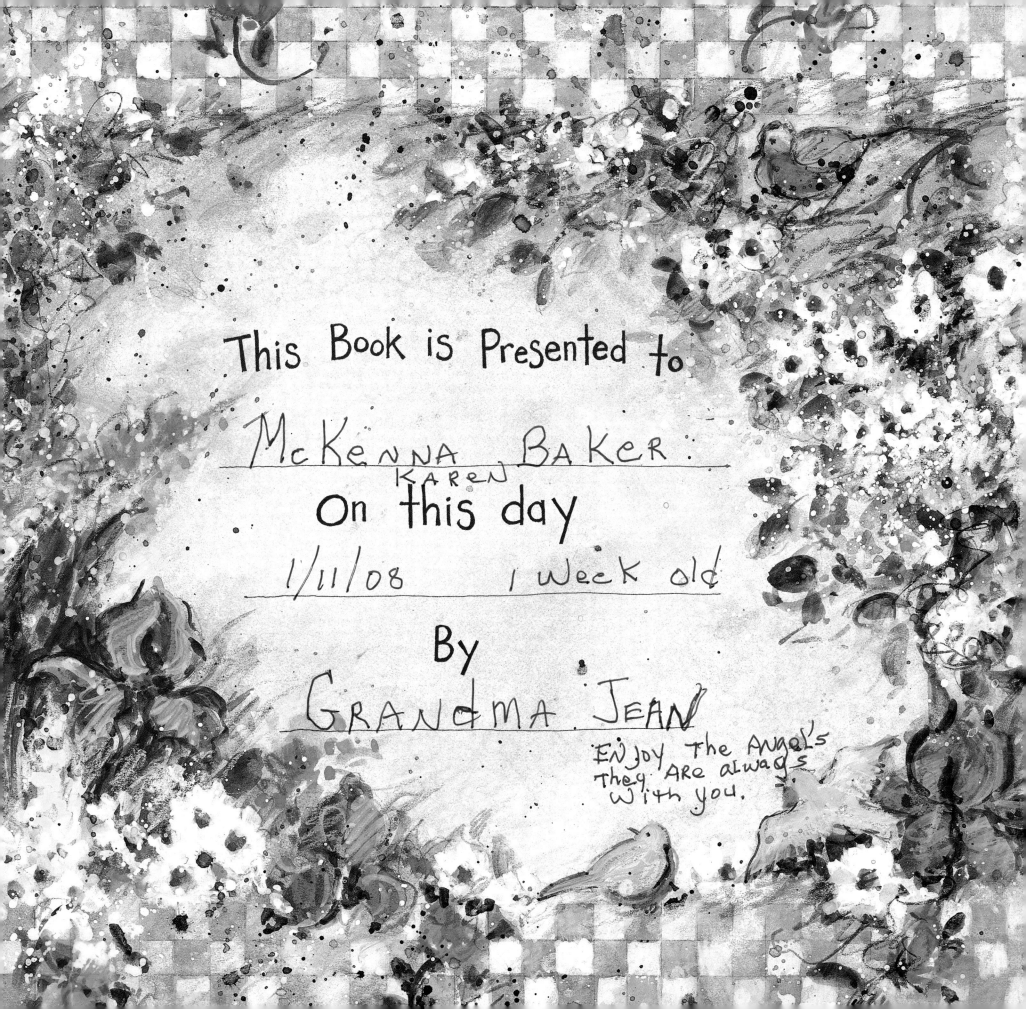

This Book is Presented to

McKenna Baker
KAREN

On this day

1/11/08   1 Week old

By

Grandma Jean

Enjoy the Angel's
they Are always
With you.

Acknowledgements

This story was inspired by the unselfish dedication of all of the care-givers of the world.

We would like to thank the creative staff at Lang Books and Winget Art for their vision and support.

Susan and Mark

To Mom, Dad and Zachary

m.k.m.

To my Mom and Mrs. Winget

s.a.w.

"Every visible thing in this world is put in the charge of an angel!"
St. Augustine

One day...
as I lay resting

In the quiet countryside,

I wakened to a wondrous sight,

A vision by my side!

Her face was fair and rosy,
Her eyes spoke peace and love,
And from her back rose feathered wings
As from a turtledove!

She was singing oh, so sweetly,
A melody so light,
Though I tried my best to keep quite still
She caught me in her sight.

She seemed to be a bit surprised
To find me with her there.
She asked if I were an angel
And what my job was here.
Of course I had to laugh at this,
An angel, what a joke!
Why, we all know that angels
Are just tales made up by folk.
She threw back her head in laughter
And clapped her hands in cheer...

And as she did this, tiny stars fell from her flowing hair.

"Then what am I, you silly thing,
If angels are not real?
How do you explain me sitting here
Beside you in this field?"

I said, "I must be dreaming,
For surely it's not true,
That mermaids swim and fairies dance
And angels watch over you!"

She kindly reached and took my hand
And brushed my weary brow,
And as she did a quietness
Passed through my soul
Somehow.

"Well, I can't speak for all unicorns
Nor mermaids in the bay.
But I tell you this
with all my heart...
Angels watch
you everyday!"

And once she had begun to talk
The meadow creatures came...
Soft brown rabbits at her feet,
Wild birds at once were tamed.

From somewhere lambs came bounding
And settled by her side.
The sun sent down her golden rays
While gentle breezes sighed.

'Seemed everyone had come to hear
The secrets she'd relay
And this is what she said to us
That fine warm
summer day:

"Please rest your eyes and listen
And soon you'll be aware
That if you just believe in us,
You'll find angels everywhere!

Now angels aren't the ones, you know,
From fairy tales of old,
Nor do we all wear halos... and
play on harps of
gold.

You'll find all of us hard working
And barely recognize
That as you live your own sweet life
We're right there by your side.

It's true, we walk your village streets
And have been known to fly,
Spreading seeds of love and joy
And peace for all mankind.

But perhaps I really should explain,
You must believe somehow,
It's rare that one of us appears
As I'm before you now.

For angels may take many forms.
It's faith that brings us here.
Look for us in simple deeds,
In thoughts that you hold dear.

We weave the silver lining
On a dark and dreary cloud.
We gather wishes on the stars
And send them heaven-bound.

Oftentimes you'll see us
In a newborn baby's smile
Or hear us in the laughter,
Of a beautiful young child.

You can feel us in the tender warmth
Of a loving family's care.
We'll help you through a troubled hour
When no one else is there.

We're the very inspiration
A painter needs to paint,
And we send a first grade teacher
The patience of a saint.

Firemen may need courage
And missionaries, zeal.
Sometimes a little miracle
Will help the sick to heal...

Or we may simply be the gentle hand
That wipes away the tear.
We give the spirit fortitude
To soothe away the fear.

Wherever we are needed
Throughout this lovely land,
You'll find an angel
strong and true
who's there to
lend a
hand."

She smiled and said, "You see my friend,
There are many ways that we appear,
As a touch, a smile, a kindred friend,
A helpful soul who's near."

With that she hugged the wooly lambs...
Sent the bunnies off to play,
She shared a gentle
smile with me
And soon was
on her
way.

I rubbed my eyes and stretched a bit
And through the midday glare,
I watched as her gossamer wings
Slowly vanished in thin air !

She rose as softly as a dream,
As graceful as a deer.
When next I turned and looked around...

Angels Were Everywhere!

Suddenly they disappeared
And bells began to peal,
The meadow rang with joy and love-
It all seemed so unreal !

Now where there once were angels,
Fragrant wildflowers grew.
The meadow grasses bowed their heads
Beneath the sky so blue..

At once the world seemed perfect,
So simple, pure and clean,
Surely a much better place
Than I had ever seen...

It was filled with love and laughter,
The beauty that I had missed.
From that day on my life was changed
And filled with heaven's bliss.

And though she never did explain
How angels come to be,
From all I'd seen and heard from her,
It's very clear to me...

They're born of
simple kindness

And love that's not denied...

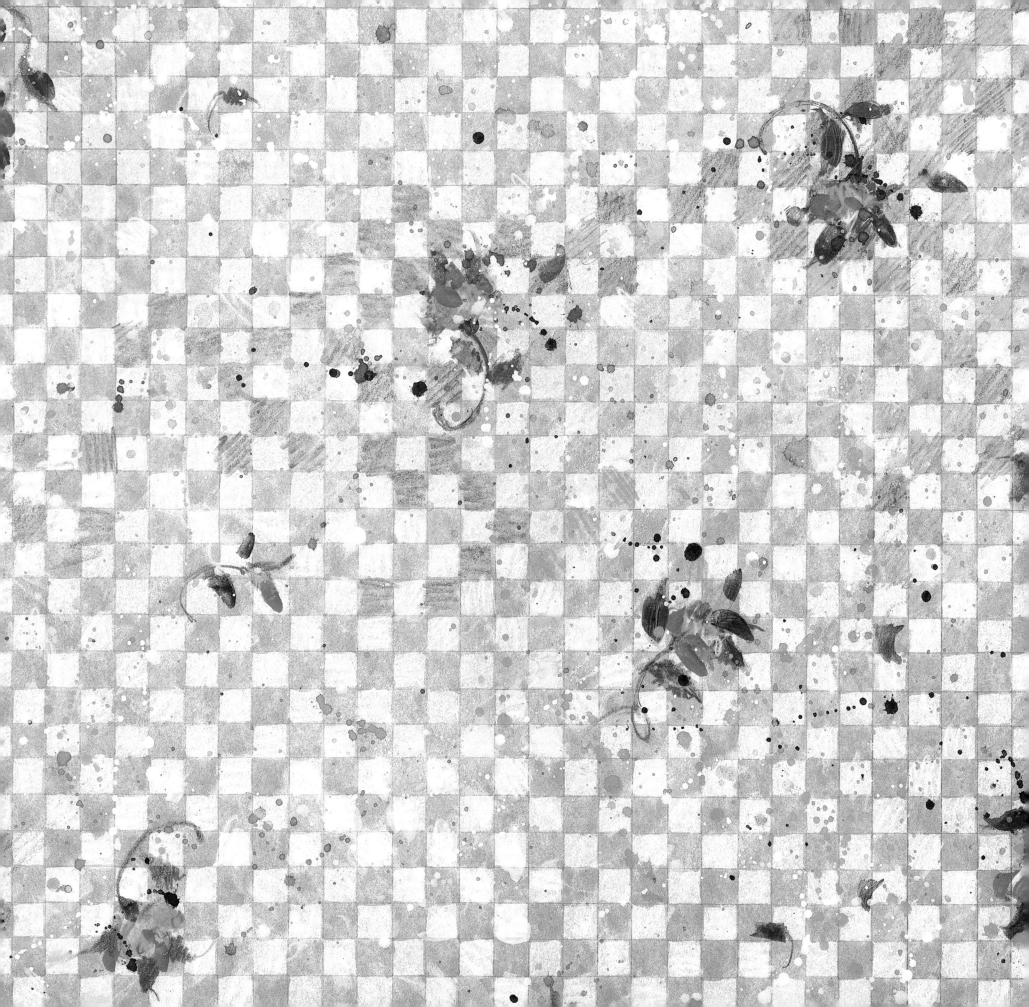